[THE LITTLE FOLKS' EDITION]
THROUGH THE LOOKING-GLASS

THROUGH THE LOOKING-GLASS AND WHAT ALICE FOUND THERE

ADAPTED FOR VERY LITTLE FOLKS FROM
THE ORIGINAL STORY

BY

LEWIS CARROLL

*WITH THIRTY-TWO ILLUSTRATIONS
BY SIR JOHN TENNIEL*

MACMILLAN CHILDREN'S BOOKS
LONDON

First edition published by Macmillan & Co. Ltd, 1903

This edition published 2016 by Macmillan Children's Books
an imprint of Pan Macmillan
20 New Wharf Road, London N1 9RR
Associated companies throughout the world
www.panmacmillan.com

ISBN: 978-1-50982-049-8

Design and typography copyright © Macmillan Children's Books 2016

1 3 5 7 9 10 8 6 4 2

A CIP catalogue record for this book is available from the British Library

Printed in China

Through the Looking-Glass and What Alice Found There,
written by Lewis Carroll, with illustrations by Sir John Tenniel,
was first published by Macmillan & Co. Ltd, 1872

NOTE

This delightful little book dates back to 1903 and was published as a companion to *The Little Folks' Edition* of *Alice's Adventures in Wonderland*. It contains only those parts of the text and illustrations from *Through the Looking-Glass and What Alice Found There* which were considered at the time to be suitable for very little children.

It is one sixth of the length of the original edition and was the first version available in full colour at a "pocket money" price.

One thing was certain, that the white kitten had nothing to do with it—it was the black kitten's fault entirely. For the white kitten had been having its face washed by the old cat for the last quarter of an hour. While Alice was sitting coiled up in a corner of an arm chair, half asleep the black kitten had been having a grand game of romps with a ball of worsted.

"Oh you wicked little thing!" cried Alice, catching up the kitten, and giving it a little kiss, to make it know that it was in disgrace. "Really Dinah ought to have taught you better manners!"

Then she scrambled back into the armchair, taking the kitten and worsted and began winding up the ball again. But she didn't get on very fast, as she was talking all the time, either to herself or the kitten.

"Do you know what tomorrow is Kitty?" Alice began. "You'd have guessed if you'd been up in the window with me. I was watching the boys getting sticks for the bonfire."

Here Alice wound two or three turns of the worsted round the kitten's neck, this led to a scramble in which the ball rolled down upon the floor, and yards and yards of it unwound again.

"Do you know I was so angry Kitty," Alice went on, as soon as they were comfortably settled again, "when I saw all the mischief you were doing, I was very nearly opening the window and putting you out into the snow.

"Do you hear the snow against the window-panes Kitty? How nice and soft it sounds! Just as if some one was kissing the window all over outside."

"Kitty can you play? Don't smile my dear, I mean it seriously. Because when we were playing just now, you watched just as if you understood—" And here I wish I could tell you half the things Alice used to say, beginning with her favourite words, "Let's pretend."

"Let's pretend that you're the Red Queen Kitty," Alice went on, as she picked the Red Queen off the table for the kitten to imitate.

"Now if you'll only attend, Kitty, and not talk so much, I'll tell you all my ideas about Looking-Glass House.

"First, there's the room you can see through the glass— that's just the same as our drawing-room, only the things go the other way. I can see all of it when I get upon a chair— all but the bit just behind the fire-place. Oh! I do wish I could see *that* bit."

"I will show you Looking-Glass House," said Alice, taking the kitten and walking into the drawing-room.

"Let's pretend the glass has got soft like gauze, so that we can get through." In another moment Alice was up on the chimney piece, and through the glass, and had jumped lightly down into Looking-Glass Room. The first thing she did was to look whether there was a fire in the fire-place.

She was quite pleased to find there was a real one blazing away.

"Oh what fun it will be when they see me through the glass in here and can't get at me."

Then she began looking about and noticed that the pictures on the wall next to the fire seemed to be alive, and the very clock on the chimney piece had got the face of a little old man, and grinned at her.

"They don't keep this so tidy as they ought to do, it is not nearly as tidy as the room I have just come out of," Alice thought to herself, as she noticed several of the chessmen down on the hearth among the cinders, but in another moment with a little, "Oh!" of surprise she was down on her hands and knees watching them. The chessmen were walking about, two and two.

"Here are the Red King and the Red Queen," Alice said (in a whisper for fear of frightening them) "and the White King and White Queen sitting on the edge of the shovel— and here are two Castles walking arm in arm— I don't think they can hear me," she went on, as she put her head closer down, "and I'm nearly sure they can't see me, I believe I'm invisible."

"It's the voice of my child!" the White Queen cried out, as she rushed past the King, so violently that she knocked him over among the cinders.

"My precious Lily! My imperial kitten!" and she began wildly scrambling up the side of the fender, to get onto the table where a white pawn lay kicking and squeaking.

"Imperial fiddlestick!" said the King, who was much annoyed by his fall.

Alice saw poor little Lily was screaming herself hoarse on the table, so she hastily picked up the Queen, and set her beside her noisy little daughter. The rapid journey through the air made the Queen gasp for breath. "Mind the Volcano," she cried out to the White King.

"What Volcano?" said the King looking anxiously up into the fire.

"Blew—me—up," panted the Queen.

Alice watched the White King, struggling from bar to bar, he'll be hours she thought, so she picked him up gently.

Alice said afterwards that she never saw such a face as the King made when he found himself being dusted and held in the air by an invisible hand.

She smoothed his hair, told him not to make such dreadful faces, and set him down gently on the table by the side of the Queen.

The King immediately fell flat on his back and lay quite still: Alice was a little alarmed, and tried to find some water to sprinkle over him, but she could see nothing but a bottle of ink, and when she got back he had recovered, and was talking to the Queen in a frightened whisper.

"I assure you, my dear," the King was saying, "I turned cold to the very ends of my whiskers!"

"Nonsense!" said the Queen, "you've got no whiskers, and you will forget it, if you don't make a note of it."

Alice looked on with great interest as the King took an enormous note book out of his pocket, and began writing. A sudden thought struck her, and she took hold of the end of the pencil, and began writing for him.

The King looked puzzled and unhappy, at last he panted out, "I must get a *thinner* pencil, I can't manage this, it writes all manner of things."

"What manner of things?" said the Queen, looking over the book (in which Alice had put, *The White Knight is sliding down the poker. He balances very badly*). "That's not a note of your feelings!"

Alice found such funny things in the King's book.

"But Oh!" she thought, suddenly jumping up, "if I don't make haste, I shall have to go back through the Looking-glass, before I've seen what the rest of the house is like! Let's have a look at the garden first!" She ran out of the room and down stairs, or at least it wasn't exactly running. She just kept the tips of her fingers on the hand-rail, and floated down without even touching the stairs.

Alice was rather glad when she got to the bottom of the stairs, and found herself walking in the natural way again.

"I should see the garden far better, if I could get to the top of that hill," she said. "Ah! here's a path leading to it." But the path did not lead straight to it, for Alice wandered up and down, until she got tired, but always came back to the house.

"It's too bad," cried Alice when for about the twentieth time, she found herself once more back at the house. "I don't believe I shall ever get into the garden." However, she started again, and this time she came to a flower-bed.

"O Tiger-lily," said Alice speaking to one that was waving gracefully about in the wind, "I *wish* you could talk!"

"We *can* talk," said the Tiger-lily.

"And can *all* flowers talk?" asked Alice.

"As well as *you* can," said the Tiger-lily.

"And much louder."

"It isn't manners for us to begin," said the Rose. "I was wondering when you'd speak! I said to myself, 'Her face has got *some* sense in it, though it's not a clever one!' But you're the right colour."

"I wish her petals curled up more," said the Tiger-lily.

"Aren't you afraid of being out here with nobody to take care of you?" said Alice.

"There's the tree in the middle," said the Rose, "if there was danger it could bark."

"It says bough-wough," cried the Daisy: "that's why all its branches are called boughs!"

Suddenly the Larkspur cried, "She's coming, I hear her footsteps, thump, thump, along the gravel walk."

Alice looked round eagerly, and found that it was the Red Queen.

By the advice of one of the flowers, Alice walked away from the Red Queen, instead of towards her, and by this means she soon found herself face to face with Her Majesty.

Alice was surprised to find that the Queen was taller than she was herself. "She was only three inches high when I found her in the ashes," she thought.

"Where are you from?" said the Red Queen. "And where are you going? Look up, speak nicely, and don't twiddle your fingers all the time."

Alice attended to all these directions, and explained that she had lost her way.

"I don't know what you mean by *your* way," said the Queen, "all ways about here belong to me— why did you come at all?" she added. "Curtsey while you're thinking, it saves time."

Alice was wondering what to do when the Red Queen said, as she looked at her watch, "It's time for you to answer now, open your mouth a little wider when you speak, and always say Your Majesty."

"I only wanted to see what the garden was like your Majesty."

The Queen took hold of Alice's hand, and they walked on in silence to the top of the hill.

"I declare it's marked out just like a chess board," said Alice. "I wish I were a chessman: of course, I should like to be a Queen best."

"So you can," said the Red Queen, "when you get to the Eighth square—" Just at this moment, somehow or other they commenced to run. The Queen went so fast that Alice could hardly keep up, still the Queen kept on crying, "*Faster!*"

The most curious thing was that the trees and other things round them never changed places at all, however fast they went.

Still the Queen cried, "Faster! Faster!" and dragged her along.

"Are we nearly there?" Alice managed to pant out at last. "Nearly there!" the Queen repeated. "We passed it ten minutes ago!"

Just when Alice was getting quite exhausted, they stopped.

"You may rest a little," said the Queen, "while I tell you how to get over the squares. You'll go two squares in the first move," she continued, "you'll get through the Third square by railway I should think. The Fourth square belongs to Tweedledum and Tweedledee, and the Fifth is mostly water, the Sixth belongs to Humpty Dumpty, the Seventh is all forest, but one of the Knights will show you the way."

"In the Eighth square," she went on, "we shall all be Queens together." Then the Red Queen suddenly vanished.

Alice started off, "I do so want to get into the Third square," she said, as she ran down the hill and jumped over the first of the six little brooks.

*   *   *   *

"Tickets, please," said the Guard, putting his head in at the window.

"Ticket child!" the Guard went on angrily. Then came a chorus of voices, "Don't keep him waiting, his time's worth a thousand pounds a minute."

"There wasn't a ticket office," said Alice. "There wasn't room for one where she came from," the chorus went on. "The land there is worth a thousand pounds an inch."

"You should have bought one from the engine-driver," said the Guard.

Then he looked at her through a pair of opera glasses and said, "You're travelling the wrong way," and went.

"So young a child," said the gentleman sitting opposite (who was dressed in paper) "should know which way she is travelling, even if she doesn't know her own name!"

"She ought to know her way to the ticket office, even if she doesn't know her alphabet," said a Goat.

Suddenly Alice felt the train give a jump in the air.

"That'll take us into the fourth square," said the Goat.

Alice was so frightened that she caught at the nearest thing, which happened to be the Goat's beard, then she knew no more until she found herself under a tree talking to a large Gnat, who was saying, "Half-way up that bush you'll see a Rocking-horse-fly, if you look."

"It's made entirely of wood, and gets about by swinging itself from branch to branch."

"What does it live on?" Alice asked eagerly.

"Sap and Sawdust," said the Gnat.

"What sort of insects do you *rejoice* in, where you come from?"

"I don't *rejoice* in insects at all," Alice explained, "because I'm rather afraid of them. But I can tell you the names of some of them."

"Of course they answer to their names?" the Gnat remarked carelessly.

"I never knew them do it," replied Alice.

"Then what's the use of their having names," said the Gnat.

"No use to *them*," said Alice, "but it's useful to the people that name them, I suppose. If not, why do they name them at all?"

"I can't say," said the Gnat, "but I should like to have a list of your insects."

"There's the Dragonfly," said Alice.

"Look on the branch above your head," said the Gnat, "and there you'll find a Snap-dragon-fly. Its body is made of plum pudding, its wings are holly-leaves, and its head is a raisin burning in brandy. It lives on mince pies and makes its nest in a Christmas-box."

"We have Butterflies," said Alice.

"There," said the Gnat, "is a Bread-and-Butter-fly."

"Its wings are thin slices of bread and butter, its body is a crust and its head is a lump of sugar. It lives on weak tea and cream."

"Supposing it couldn't find any?" said Alice.

"Then it would die."

"But that must happen very often," said Alice thoughtfully.

"It always happens," said the Gnat.

After this the Gnat went, so Alice got up and walked on.

Soon Alice came to a dark wood, which she felt a little timid about going into.

"I must go through this wood to get to the Eighth square, and then I shall be a Queen," she said to herself.

"This must be the wood," thought Alice, "where things have no names. I wonder what will become of my name, I shouldn't like to lose it.

"It looks nice and cool under the—"

"This," she said putting her hand on the trunk of a tree. Such a funny thing had happened, Alice had forgotten her own name, and the name of everything else as well.

Just then a Fawn came wandering by: it looked at Alice with its large gentle eyes.

"What do you call yourself?" said the Fawn.

"Nothing just now," she answered rather sadly.

"Please would you tell me what you call yourself?" she said timidly. "I think that might help a little."

"I'll tell you if you come a little further on," said the Fawn.

So they walked on together through the wood, Alice with her arms clasped lovingly round the soft neck of the Fawn. When they came to an open field, the Fawn gave a bound into the air.

"I'm a Fawn!" it cried out in a voice of delight, and then darted away at full speed.

Alice went on and on a long way, but wherever the road divided, there was sure to be two finger-posts pointing the same way, one said, "To Tweedledum's House," and the other, "To The House of Tweedledee."

"I do believe" said Alice at last, "that they live in the same house."

She wandered on, when turning a sharp corner, she came upon two fat little men. They were standing under a tree, each with an arm round the other's neck, and Alice knew which was which in a moment, because one of them had 'DUM' on his collar, and the other 'DEE'. "I suppose they've each got 'TWEEDLE', round at the back of the collar," she said to herself.

They stood so still, she forgot they were alive.

"If you think we're wax-works," said the one marked 'Dum', "you ought to pay."

"And, if you think we're alive, you ought to speak," said the one marked 'Dee'.

"I'm sure I'm very sorry," was all Alice could say. She kept thinking of the old song:

"Tweedledum and Tweedledee
    Agreed to have a battle;
For Tweedledum said Tweedledee
    Had spoiled his nice new rattle.
Just then flew down a monstrous crow,
    As black as a tar-barrel;
Which frightened both the heroes so,
    They quite forgot their quarrel."

"You've begun wrong!" cried Tweedledum. "The first thing in a visit is to say, 'How d'ye do?' and shake hands!"

And here the two brothers gave each other a hug, and held out the two free hands.

Alice took hold of both hands at once, and the next moment they were dancing round in a ring.

"Four times round is enough for one dance," Tweedledum panted out, and they left off suddenly.

Just then Alice was alarmed by hearing a great noise like the puffing of a steam engine in the wood.

"Are there lions and tigers about here?" she asked timidly.

"It's only the Red King snoring," said Tweedledee.

"Come and look at him!" the brothers cried, as they each took one of Alice's hands and led her to where the King was sleeping.

"Isn't he a *lovely* sight?" said Tweedledum.

Alice couldn't say honestly that he was. He had a tall red night-cap on, with a tassel, and he was lying crumpled up into a sort of untidy heap, snoring loudly.

"What do you think he is dreaming about?" said Tweedledee.

Alice said, "Nobody can guess that."

"Why about *you*, and if he left off dreaming, you'd be nowhere," he said.

"You'd go bang! if he woke,"

said Tweedledum.

"I shouldn't," said Alice indignantly, and she began to cry.

"Do you think it's going to rain?" said Tweedledum, opening a large umbrella.

"It may rain outside, if it chooses, we've no objection," said Tweedledee.

"Selfish things!" thought Alice, and she was just going to say, "Good night" and leave them, when Tweedledum sprang out from under the umbrella and seized her by the wrist.

"Do you see that?" he said, in a voice choking with passion, and his eyes grew large and yellow in a moment, as he pointed with a trembling finger at a small white thing lying under the tree.

"It's only a rattle," said Alice, after a careful examination of the little white thing. "Not a rattle-*snake*, you know," she added hastily, thinking that he was frightened: "only an old rattle—old and broken."

"I knew it was!" cried Tweedledum, stamping about wildly and tearing his hair. "It's spoilt of course!" Here he looked at Tweedledee, who immediately tried to hide himself under the umbrella.

"You needn't be so angry about an old rattle," said Alice soothingly.

"But it isn't old! It's new I tell you— I bought it yesterday— My nice new RATTLE!" and his voice rose to a perfect scream.

"Of course you agree to a battle?" said Tweedledum to Tweedledee, who was trying to fold himself up in the umbrella.

"I suppose so," was the sulky reply, "only *she* must help us to dress up."

So the two brothers went off hand-in-hand into the wood, and returned in a few minutes with their arms full of things—such as bolsters, blankets, hearth-rugs, tablecloths, dish-covers, and coal-scuttles.

"I hope you're good at pinning, and tying strings," remarked Tweedledum.

"Really they'll be more like bundles of old clothes than anything else," thought Alice, as she tied a bolster round Tweedledee's neck, to keep his head from being cut off.

"You know," he added gravely, "it's one of the most serious things that can possibly happen to one in battle, to get one's head cut off."

Alice laughed loud, but managed to turn it into a cough, for fear of hurting his feelings.

"Do I look very pale?" said Tweedledum, coming to have the saucepan he called a helmet, tied on.

"Well— yes— a *little*," Alice replied gently.

"I've got the headache!" said Tweedledum, "and I've got the toothache!" said Tweedledee.

"Don't fight today," said Alice.

"We must fight a bit, but I don't care about going on long, suppose we fight till six o'clock, and then have dinner," said Tweedledum. "There's only one sword," he continued, "but you can have the umbrella— It's quite as sharp, we must be quick. It's getting as dark as it can."

"It's the crow!" cried Tweedledee, in a shrill voice of alarm, and the two brothers took to their heels and were soon out of sight.

Alice ran under a large tree, for the wind was blowing hard.

"Why, here's somebody's shawl being blown away," she said, and she caught it as she spoke.

In another moment the White Queen came running wildly through the wood.

"How dreadfully untidy she is," thought Alice, as she went civilly up to her, and asked to be allowed to put her straight, her hair *was* so untidy.

"The hair-brush got entangled in it," said the Queen with a sigh. Alice found the brush, and did her best to get the hair into order.

"You look better now," she said, "but you really ought to have a lady's maid."

"I'm sure I'll take you with pleasure!" the Queen said.

"Twopence a week, and jam every other day."

Alice laughed and said, "I don't want you to hire *me*, and I don't like jam.

"I don't want any *today* at any rate."

"You couldn't have it if you *did* want it," the Queen said. "The rule is jam tomorrow, jam yesterday, but never today."

"I can't understand," said Alice, "it's dreadfully confusing!"

"Ah! you should live backwards," said the Queen, "then one's memory works both ways."

"Mine only works one way," said Alice.

"That's a poor sort of memory," the Queen remarked. "I remember things best, that happened the week after next. Now the King's Messenger. He's in prison now, being punished, and the trial doesn't even begin until next Wednesday: and of course the crime comes last of all."

"Suppose he never commits the crime?" said Alice. "I don't see why he should be punished."

"You're wrong *there*," said the Queen: "Were you ever punished?"

"Only for faults," said Alice.

"And it did you good, I know. Now, how old are you?" continued the Queen.

"I'm seven and a half exactly," said Alice.

"You needn't say 'exactually'," the Queen remarked. "Now I'm just one hundred and one, five months and a day."

"I can't believe *that*," said Alice.

"Try again, shut your eyes and draw a long breath," said the Queen.

"It's no use, I can't believe impossible things," said Alice.

"You've had no practice," said the Queen. "When I was your age, I've believed as many as six hundred impossible things before breakfast."

Just at this moment a gust of wind came, and blew the Queen's shawl across a little brook. The Queen ran after it and Alice followed her.

"I've got it, I've got it," she cried in a triumphant tone, the last word ended in a bleat so like a sheep that Alice quite started.

She looked at the Queen, who suddenly seemed to have wrapped herself up in wool. Alice rubbed her eyes. She couldn't make out what had happened. Was she in a shop? And was that *really* a sheep that was sitting on the other side of the counter.

"What do you want to buy?" the Sheep said at last.

"I don't *quite* know yet," Alice said gently. "I should like to look all round first."

"You may look in front of you, and on both sides if you like," said the Sheep, "but you can't look *all* round you, unless you've got eyes at the back of your head."

As Alice had not she contented herself with looking at the shelves as she came to them.

"How much are the eggs, please?" she said timidly.

"Fivepence farthing for one— twopence for two," the Sheep replied.

"Then two are cheaper than one?" said Alice in a surprised tone.

"Only you *must* eat both, if you buy two," said the Sheep.

"Then I'll have *one* please," said Alice, as she put her money down on the counter; "for perhaps they are not nice."

"You must take the egg yourself," said the Sheep as she set it upright on a shelf.

As Alice walked towards it, the egg got larger and larger, and more and more human: when she came nearer to it she found it had eyes and nose and mouth, and when she was quite close to it, she saw clearly that it was HUMPTY DUMPTY himself.

"How exactly like an egg he is," said Alice aloud.

"It's *very* provoking," Humpty Dumpty said, "to be called an egg."

"Some eggs are very pretty," said Alice hoping to compliment him.

"Some people have no more sense than a baby," said Humpty.

"Do you know Tweedle-dee?" asked Alice. "He repeated some very nice poetry to me."

"*I* can repeat poetry as well as other folk, if it comes to that—"

"Oh it needn't come to that!" said Alice hastily; but it was too late, he raised his voice and began—

"I sent a message to the fish:
I told them 'This is what I wish.'
The little fishes of the sea,
They sent an answer back to me.
The little fishes' answer was
'We cannot do it, Sir, because—'
I sent to them again to say,
'It will be better to obey.'
The fishes answered with a grin,
'Why, what a temper you are in!'"

"That's all," said Humpty Dumpty. "Good-bye," and he disappeared.

Alice was just thinking how stupid Humpty Dumpty was, when there was a loud crash, and Soldiers came rushing in every direction, so that Alice was very glad to get into an open place, where she found the White King. At the same moment a Messenger arrived, he was so out of breath that he could only wave his hand and make dreadful faces.

"You alarm me," said the King. "I feel faint— give me a ham sandwich."

Much to Alice's amuse-ment, the Messenger opened his bag and handed the King a sandwich, which he ate.

"Another," said the King.

"There's only hay left," said the Messenger.

"Hay then," the King faintly murmured.

"Nothing like eating hay when you're faint," he remarked as he munched away.

"They're at it again," shouted the Messenger in the King's ear.

"Who are at it again?" Alice ventured to ask.

"Why the Lion and the Unicorn of course," said the King. "They are fighting for the crown; and the best of the joke is that it is my crown. Let's run and see them," and they trotted off, Alice repeating the words,

"The Lion and the Unicorn were
fighting for the Crown:
The Lion beat the Unicorn
all round the town.
Some gave them white bread
and some gave them brown;
Some gave them plum-cake and
drummed them out of town."

Presently they came to a great crowd, in the midst of which the Lion and the Unicorn were fighting.

They placed themselves close to where Hatta, the other Messenger, was watching the fight, with a cup of tea in one hand and a piece of bread and butter in the other.

"He's only just out of prison, and he hadn't finished his tea when he was sent in," the Hare whispered to Alice.

"He's very hungry and thirsty you see, because they only give them oyster-shells in there. How are you, dear child?" he went on, putting his arm affectionately round Hatta's neck.

Hatta looked round and nodded, and went on with his bread-and-butter.

"I suppose they'll soon bring the white bread and the brown?" Alice remarked.

"It's waiting for 'em now," said Hatta, "this is a bit of it I'm eating."

There was a pause in the fight, and the Hare and Hatta carried round trays of white and brown bread. Alice took a piece, but found it very dry.

At this moment the Unicorn sauntered by, with his hands in his pockets. "I had the best of it this time," he said.

"A little, a little," the King replied nervously.

"I always thought there was no such things as Unicorns," said Alice.

"And I always thought there was no such things as children," said the Unicorn. "Now if you'll believe in me, I'll believe in you. Is that a bargain?"

"If you like," said Alice.

"Come, fetch out the plum-cake, old man," said the Unicorn turning from her to the King.

The Hare took a cake out of his bag and handed it to Alice.

The Lion joined them while this was going on.

"What's this?" he said, blinking lazily at Alice.

"You'll *never* guess," cried the Unicorn eagerly. "I couldn't."

"Are you animal, or vegetable, or mineral?" he said, yawning.

"It's not a real thing" said the Unicorn. "Then hand round the plum cake," said the Lion.

The King was so nervous when he sat between them, that his crown was nearly shaking off his head.

"I should win easy if we fought for the Crown *now!*" said the Lion.

"I'm not so sure of that," said the Unicorn.

"Why I beat you all round the town, you chicken!" said the Lion angrily.

"I say, this isn't fair," cried the Unicorn, "she's given the Lion twice as much as me."

"She's kept none for herself anyhow," said the Lion. "Do you like plum-cake?"

Before Alice could answer, the drums began. Where the noise came from she could not make out, the air seemed full of it, and it rang through and through her head, till she felt quite deafened. She started to her feet, and in her terror she sprang across the brook, and had just time to see the Lion and the Unicorn rise to their feet with angry looks at being interrupted.

"If that doesn't drum them out of town," thought Alice, "nothing ever will," and she was wondering what she should do next, when she heard a great shouting, and saw the Red Knight galloping down upon her, brandishing a great club.

"You're my prisoner," he shouted as he tumbled off his horse.

He mounted again, and as soon as he was seated, he shouted, "You're my—"

But here another voice broke in, "Ahoy! Ahoy!" and Alice saw it was the White Knight riding up. When he got opposite the Red Knight, they both sat staring at one another.

"She's *my* prisoner, you know!" said the Red Knight.

"Yes, but I came and rescued her," the White Knight replied.

"Well, we must fight for her then," said the Red Knight as he took up his helmet and put it on.

"You will observe the Rules of Battle, of course?" the White Knight said, putting on his helmet too.

"I always do," said the Red Knight, and they began banging away at each other with such fury that Alice got behind a tree to be out of the way of the blows. At last they both fell off on their heads, side by side; then they got up, shook hands, the Red Knight mounted and galloped off.

"May I help you off with your helmet?" said Alice to the White Knight.

"Thanks," he answered as Alice took it off for him, "and now, help me on my horse and I will see you to the end of the wood."

The Knight had all kinds of queer things tied to his saddle, and he was certainly not a good rider, as you will see if you look at the first picture in this book.

At last, after the Knight had tumbled off his horse on to his head, ever so many times, they came to the end of the wood. They shook hands, then he rode slowly away. Alice watched him tumbling off first on one side, then on the other. After the fourth or fifth tumble, he reached a turn, then she waved her handkerchief to him, and he was soon out of sight.

A few steps brought her to the edge of a brook. "The Eighth square at last!" she cried as she bounded over, and threw herself down to rest on a lawn as soft as moss. "Oh! how glad I am to be here! And what is this on my head?" she exclaimed. "How can it have got there?" She put up her hands and lifted something off, now what *do* you think it was. Why, a lovely golden crown.

III

"Well this *is* grand!" said Alice. "I never expected to be a Queen so soon."

She got up and walked about, rather stiffly at first, for fear the crown might fall off. Everything was happening so strangely that she was not at all surprised to find the Red Queen and the White Queen, one sitting on each side of her.

"Please would you tell me—" she began, looking timidly at the Red Queen.

"Speak when you're spoken to," interrupted the Red Queen sharply.

"If everybody obeyed that rule," said Alice, "nobody would ever speak."

"Ridiculous!" cried the Queen. "What right have you to call yourself a Queen, you've passed no examination?"

Then the two Queens began asking Alice all sorts of unanswerable questions.

"Sing the White Queen a lullaby," said the Red Queen.

"I don't know one," said Alice.

"I must do it myself," said the Red Queen, and she began:

"Hush-a-by lady, in Alice's lap!
Till the feast's ready, we've time
for a nap:
When the feast's over, we'll go
to the ball—
Red Queen, and White Queen,
and Alice, and all!"

When she had finished she put her head down on Alice's shoulder. "I'm getting sleepy too," she said. In a moment both Queens were asleep and snoring loudly.

"What *am* I to do?" exclaimed Alice, looking about as first one round head, and then the other rolled down from her shoulder, and lay like a heavy lump in her lap.

"I don't think it ever happened before that anyone had to take care of two Queens asleep at once! No, not in all the History of England— It couldn't you know, because there never was more than one Queen at a time."

Alice felt more and more hot, and uncomfortable.

"Do wake up, you heavy things!" she went on in an impatient tone, but there was no answer but a gentle snoring.

The snoring got more distinct every moment, and sounded more like a tune: at last she could even make out words, and she listened so eagerly that, when the two great heads suddenly vanished from her lap, she hardly missed them.

She was standing before an arched doorway, over which were the words QUEEN ALICE in large letters. Presently the door opened a little way, and a creature with a long beak put its head out and said, "No admittance till the week after next," and then shut the door with a bang.

After this an old Frog hobbled up.

"What is it now?" he said in a hoarse whisper.

"Where's the servant whose business it is to answer the door?" she began.

"To answer the door?" he said. "What's it been asking for?"

"I don't know what you mean," she said.

"I speaks English, doesn't I?" the Frog went on, "or are you deaf? What did it ask for?"

"Nothing!" said Alice impatiently. "I've been knocking at it."

As the door opened a shrill voice was heard singing:

"To the Looking-Glass world it
was Alice that said
'I've a sceptre in hand, I've a
crown on my head;
Let the Looking-Glass creatures
whatever they be,
Come and dine with the Red Queen,
the White Queen, and me!' "

Then came the chorus:

"Then fill up the glasses as quick
as you can,
And sprinkle the table with
buttons and bran:
Put cats in the coffee, and mice
in the tea—
And welcome Queen Alice with
thirty-times-three!"

There were about fifty guests. Some were animals, some birds, and a few flowers.

Alice sat in an empty chair between the Red and the White Queens.

"You've missed the soup and fish," the Red Queen began, "let me introduce you to the leg of mutton. Alice— Mutton, Mutton—Alice." The leg of mutton got up from the dish and made a little bow.

"May I cut you a slice?" said Alice.

"Certainly not," said the Red Queen, "you should never cut anyone you have been introduced to."

"Take care of yourself!" screamed the White Queen seizing Alice by the hair with both hands. "Something's going to happen." And true enough, all sorts of things did happen in a moment. The candles all grew up to the ceiling, the plates and cruets flew away, the soup ladle was walking up the table to Alice.

"I can't stand this any longer," she cried, as she seized the table cloth with both hands: one good pull, and plates, dishes, guests, and candles came crashing in a heap on the floor. "And as for *you*," she went on, turning fiercely on the Red Queen, whom she considered the cause of all the mischief— but the Queen had dwindled down to the size of a little doll and was trying to escape.

"As for *you*," Alice repeated, as she caught hold of her. "I'll shake you like a kitten!"

The Red Queen made no resistance, only her face grew very small, and her eyes got very large and green: and as Alice went on shaking her she kept on growing shorter— and fatter— and softer— and rounder— and—, and it really was a kitten, after all.

"Your Red Majesty shouldn't purr so loudly," Alice said rubbing her eyes, and addressing the kitten with some severity.

"You woke me out of— Oh! such a nice dream! And you've been along with me Kitty— all through the Looking-Glass world. Did you know it dear?"

But the kitten only purred.

THE END